JOSEPH'S BIG RIDE

TERRY FARISH   Art by KEN DALEY

annick press
toronto + berkeley + vancouver

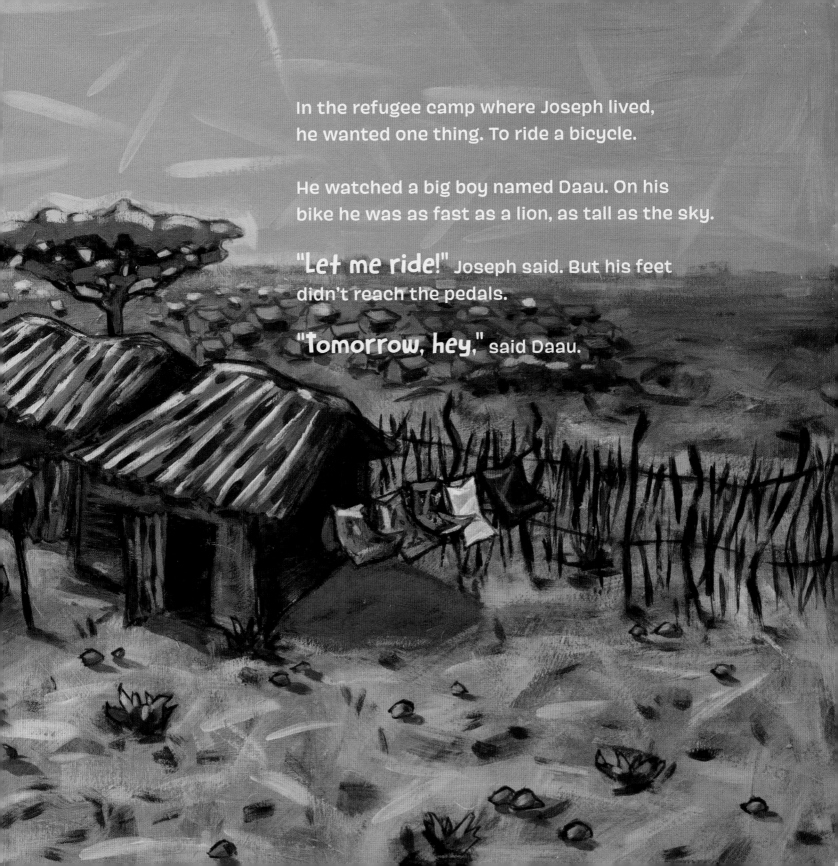

In the refugee camp where Joseph lived,
he wanted one thing. To ride a bicycle.

He watched a big boy named Daau. On his
bike he was as fast as a lion, as tall as the sky.

"Let me ride!" Joseph said. But his feet
didn't reach the pedals.

"Tomorrow, hey," said Daau.

Joseph loved to help Daau fix his bike. He fetched screwdrivers, twisted the handlebars, pumped when a tire went flat. And he waited for his legs to grow long.

Every day Daau told him, **"Tomorrow, hey."**

But then Joseph and his mama traveled far from the camp. They did not walk. They did not pedal. They flew on an airplane all the way to America.

Joseph did not forget the bicycle.

In America, Mama and Joseph live in an apartment. Joseph watches this new world out the window. He hears basketballs, **pat-tap-a-tap**. He sees streetlights instead of a sky full of stars. He smells new food that is not like his mother's lentil stew.

One morning, he shouts, **"Mama, look!"**

Beside a railing is a small red bicycle.
They both lean out the window. Joseph says,
"On this bike my feet would touch the pedals."

But Mama hauls him back. "We must prepare.
School is tomorrow."

Joseph pictures the schoolroom the way it was
at Kakuma, with one hundred children all shouting
words the teacher writes on the blackboard.

Here, he would not know the teacher.

Here, he would not know the children.

He would rather stay home with the bike.

Mama has none
of that. She marches
Joseph out the door on the
first day of school. On the way,
they see a girl with a **whoosh** of big,
curly hair whirl past them on the red bicycle.

"Are you going to my school?" Whoosh calls. She points,
and he sees a building long like a river. But his mind is on the bike.
He will go to school, he decides, because the bike is going there.

In his class, Joseph does not find one hundred children. He counts, "One, two, three ..." When he gets to eighteen he recognizes the hair. It's Whoosh.

Through the window, he sees her bike. He is happy to see it, and sits.

At the end of the day, he races home behind it.

At Joseph's apartment building, Whoosh drops the bicycle.
She climbs backward up the stairs. She lives here, too!

"What's your name?" she calls.

Joseph ignores her and kneels by the bike. **"Tomorrow, hey,"**
he says, the words Daau told him. "I will ride you."

"Tomorrow Hey!" Whoosh laughs.
"Is that your name? I like that."
He does not answer.
He is thinking about
how to get a ride
on this bike.

Joseph decides to give
Whoosh something of great value
in exchange for a ride. He draws a lion.
Sleek and fast. In the morning, he tucks it
between the spokes of the small red bicycle.

Then he watches. His turn is coming!

Whoosh blasts down the stairs.
Spots the paper and unrolls the lion.

Joseph comes to claim his ride.

"Okay!" she says.
She flings her arms wide.
"We can be friends."

"Friends?" Joseph is surprised.

Whoosh gets on the
bike. Throws him a smile.
Waves the lion in the wind.

"I gave you the lion for a ride
on ..." Joseph begins.

Whooop. She is gone.

He did not even get to touch the bike.

"Tomorrow, hey," Joseph says
as he slowly walks to school.

Joseph watches at the window. A new smell he likes, pizza, wafts through the screen. He hears the basketball bounce on the blacktop–boys are shooting hoops by streetlight. His mind, though, returns to the small red bike.

The next day Joseph waits in the bike's parking space, his bandanna in his hand.

Whoosh slides down the railing.

"Please I want to ride the bike," he says. "You may wear this. It holds your hair in the wind."

"Want to see?"

Joseph follows her to a toolshed. His mouth is an **O** of wonder at so many tools. The bike is twisted and bent.

His heart is racing. He has seen bikes worse than this. His hands itch to pick up a tool. "I have fixed bikes," he says. He looks at Whoosh.

She shrugs.

He picks up a wrench.
Remembers how to loosen a bolt.

Holds tight to the handlebars. Gives
them a tug so they face frontward.

It is beautiful. This bike.
The seat. The pedals.
The spokes.

He **straightens** the fender.

Presses the pump on the valve.
Pushes air in the tire.

With his bandanna he shines the bike's
red body. "Ohhhhh," Whoosh sings.
"You fixed it."

Joseph's chest
sparks with pride.

"Want a ride?"
she says.

He grabs the handlebars, wheels the bike out. It is happening! He sweeps his leg over the seat. His foot finds the pedal as he rolls fast down a slope. He swerves to avoid a tree. The bike dumps him.

"Those trees," Whoosh says.

Joseph gets up, mortified. He
doesn't know **HOW** to ride a bike.

He swings his leg over the top
again. Pushes the pedal down.
Falls. Gets back on. Crashes again.

And again.

Then he is pedaling. He makes it as far as the sidewalk.

Then he balances all the way down the slope.

Now he feels the
rhythm of the bike.
He leans back and laughs.

This is how Daau must have felt
when he rode his bike in the camp.

He sees Whoosh jumping up and down.

"I am riding, Whoosh," he shouts.

"You call me **Whoosh?**" she shouts back. "Not as
funny as Tomorrow Hey."

"You call me Tomorrow Hey?"

This makes Joseph laugh so hard he and
the bike tumble over with his laughing.

And then Whoosh falls down laughing, too.

"I rode the bike," he shouts.
A smile lights his face.

The bike! He jumps up. He lifts it.
Brushes leaves off the seat
and the fender.

Then Tomorrow Hey
and Whoosh take turns
riding till the round
moon rises above.

Edited by Debbie Rogosin
Designed by Belle Wuthrich
The artwork for this book was created with acrylic
and marker on illustration board.

Annick Press Ltd.

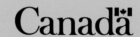

We acknowledge the support of the Canada Council for the Arts, the Ontario Arts Council,
and the participation of the Government of Canada/la participation du gouvernement du
Canada for our publishing activities.

ONTARIO ARTS COUNCIL
CONSEIL DES ARTS DE L'ONTARIO
an Ontario government agency
un organisme du gouvernement de l'Ontario

Funded by the
Government
of Canada

Financé par le
gouvernement
du Canada

Canada

Cataloging in Publication
Farish, Terry, author
    Joseph's big ride / Terry Farish ; art by Ken Daley.

Issued in print and electronic formats.
ISBN 978-1-55451-806-7 (bound).—ISBN 978-1-55451-805-0 (paperback).—
ISBN 978-1-55451-807-4 (html).—ISBN 978-1-55451-808-1 (pdf)

I. Daley, Ken, 1976–, illustrator II. Title.

PZ7.F22713Jo 2016   j813'.54   C2015-905369-2
                                              C2015-905370-6

Distributed in Canada by University of Toronto Press.
Published in the U.S.A. by Annick Press (U.S.) Ltd.
Distributed in the U.S.A. by Publishers Group West.

Printed in China

Visit us at: www.annickpress.com
Visit Terry Farish at: terryfarish.com
Visit Ken Daley at: kendaleyart.com

Also available in e-book format.
Please visit www.annickpress.com/ebooks.html for more details. Or scan

For Moses
–T.F.

To my wife, Nadine,
and to all the children
of the world: I hope this
story will inspire you to
believe in yourself and
reach for greatness!
–K.D.